THE EXTRAORDINARY FILES

Ghost in the Screen

Paul Blum

RISING ★ STAR

nasen
Helping Everyone Achieve
■ ■■■ ■■ nasen

NASEN House, 4/5 Amber Business Village, Amber Close,
Amington, Tamworth, Staffordshire B77 4RP

Rising Stars UK Ltd.
22 Grafton Street, London W1S 4EX
www.risingstars-uk.com

Published 2007

Cover design: Button plc
Illustrator: Enzo Troiano
Text design and typesetting: pentacorbig
Publisher: Gill Budgell
Editor: Maoliosa Kelly
Editorial consultants: Lorraine Petersen and Cliff Moon

British Library Cataloguing in Publication Data.
A CIP record for this book is available from the British Library.

ISBN: 978 1 84680 253 9

Printed by Craft Print International Limited, Singapore

CHAPTER ONE

In the middle of the night, an 11-year-old girl woke up. She was having a nightmare. It was the same nightmare she had every night. In it, she saw a girl with long hair. The girl was screaming and trying to turn the handle of a locked door.

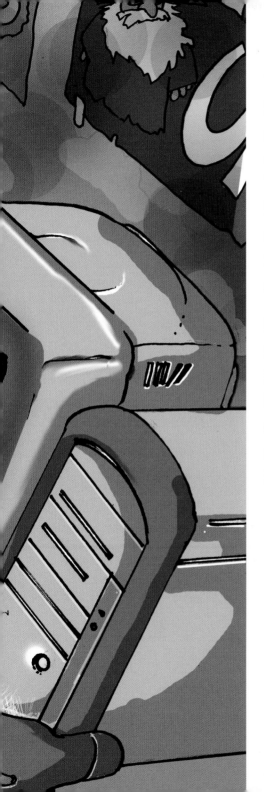

Tracy got out of bed.
She turned on her
computer but she didn't
download any software.
The girl with the long
hair appeared on the
screen. There was a
terrible sound
of screaming.

Night after night,
the same thing
happened, but Tracy
kept the nightmares a
secret. Before long,
she became ill from
lack of sleep.

Tracy lived with her grandmother, Mrs Stevens. Tracy's mum had died when she was a baby. Mrs Stevens had never liked her granddaughter. She just put up with having to look after her.

When Tracy became ill, Mrs Stevens said she was going mad. She took her to doctors for tests, but they couldn't help.

Every time they tried to get her to sleep, the computers she was linked to crashed.

Then the Government heard about Tracy and wanted to find out why she made computers crash.

They thought she could be a threat to national security.

CHAPTER TWO

MI5 Headquarters, Vauxhall, London

Laura Turnbull and Robert Parker were British Secret Service Agents. They worked for MI5. They were in the office of Commander Watson, their boss.

"I want you to find out as much as you can about Tracy," he said. "An 11-year-old girl who can make computers crash is quite something! You will live with the family for a few weeks and report back."

"Oh no! I hate kids," said Turnbull to Parker. "I'm not going to enjoy this. I don't ever want to be a mum."

The two agents went to Tracy's house and
Mrs Stevens showed them to their room.
She was glad to let the two agents stay.
She hoped that when they left, they would
take Tracy away with them.

Agent Turnbull wanted to know where Tracy was.

"I keep the little madam locked in her bedroom,"
said Mrs Stevens.

Mrs Stevens unlocked Tracy's bedroom door.
Tracy was lying face down on her pillow.

"Here she is. Good luck to you, Agent Turnbull,
you'll need it with this one," the old woman said.

She gave Turnbull the key to the door.

There was a long silence. Turnbull waited for Tracy to say something, but she turned away. After ten minutes Turnbull said, "That grandma of yours is out of order, the way she treats you."

Tracy turned round to look at Turnbull.

"Locking you in your bedroom is wrong," said Turnbull.

"Do you think so?" Tracy asked.

"I most certainly do!" Agent Turnbull said.

"Grandma says I get on her nerves," said Tracy. "She says she's sick to death of me."

Turnbull got up and walked around the room. She looked at Tracy's toys.

"Do you collect dolls?" she asked. "These ones look pretty old."

"They belonged to my mum," Tracy said.

"Tell me about her."

"I can't. She died when I was a baby," Tracy sobbed.

"I'm sorry," said Turnbull. "My mum died when I was seven. I'll never get over it either."

They had broken the ice. Tracy felt she could trust Agent Turnbull. So she told Turnbull her secret.

She told her about her
nightmares and about
the long-haired girl
on the computer screen.

Turnbull took a risk.
She gave Tracy
the bedroom key.

"If you see her tonight,
come and wake me up,"
she said.

CHAPTER THREE

Turnbull went back to her room. Parker was working on his laptop and there were files everywhere.

"I see you've made yourself at home," she groaned. "This room's almost as messy as your office."

"I've logged on to some data about Mrs Stevens," he said. "Her daughter Julie died in a terrible accident. The girl was in the bath and all the windows in the room were shut. There was a gas leak from the water heater. She passed out and drowned."

Turnbull was shocked.

"It happened in the bathroom of this house," said Parker.

"How awful!" said Turnbull, with a shiver. "I don't think we'll get much sleep tonight I may need to go and see Tracy in the middle of the night."

"What for? A midnight feast?" he joked.

"No, to see the ghost in her computer," she answered.

Parker wanted to know more but Turnbull said, "It's a secret."

It was three o'clock in the morning when Tracy woke Turnbull up. Parker was already awake.

"Come with me, Laura. I've had the dream," said Tracy.

Turnbull went with Tracy. Parker waited a few minutes and then followed them.

Tracy turned on the computer as Turnbull watched. The girl with long hair appeared on the screen. She looked very frightened and was screaming and crying. The girl was trying to escape from her room but the doors and windows were locked. Something was creeping up on her. Then the screen went blank.

"That's incredible!" said Turnbull.

Tracy turned the computer on again but the picture of the girl had gone.

Just then, Parker knocked at the door.

"Are you two all right?" he asked.

"Yes," said Turnbull. "But we have a little problem."

They told him about the ghost on the screen.
Parker worked at the computer but he couldn't
get the pictures back. There was nothing in the
computer's memory.

Mrs Stevens had come into the bedroom. She wanted to know what all the fuss was about.

"Mrs Stevens, what do you know about a frightened young woman with long hair who is locked in a room?" asked Turnbull.

"I don't know what you're talking about. But I want you and your sidekick out of my house tomorrow morning. You're not helping Tracy, you're making her worse!"

"But Tracy and I saw ..." Turnbull began.

"I don't care what you saw," Mrs Stevens screamed. "You're detectives, aren't you? Haven't you worked it out yet? Tracy is mad!"

Tracy began to cry.

Turnbull comforted Tracy and stayed with her until she went to sleep. Then she went back to her room. Parker wanted to talk about what Turnbull had seen on the computer screen but she was too tired.

"It's too late now," she said, getting into bed. "I'll be able to think more clearly in the morning."

"I have work to do," he said. "There are some leads to follow up."

"You mean you're going to tap away on your computer all night," she said. "You can tell me all about it when you bring me a cup of tea in a few hours time."

That night neither Parker nor Mrs Stevens slept.
The old woman walked up and down in her room.

She was worried about the girl with long hair in a locked room. How much did Tracy know? She decided it was time to shut her granddaughter's mouth, once and for all.

CHAPTER FOUR

When Turnbull woke up, Parker gave her a cup of tea and showed her some photographs.

"Do you know who this is?" he asked.

"It's the girl on the computer," she said.

"That's what I thought you'd say!" Parker said. "This is Julie Stevens, Tracy's mum. She was 20 years old when she died."

"Didn't you say she drowned?" asked Turnbull.

"Yes," said Parker. "But the case was never closed. The police weren't happy about it. Mrs Steven's daughter, Julie, had just had a baby but she wasn't married."

"So she was going to be a single mum?" asked Turnbull.

"Yes, and in Mrs Steven's eyes, that made her a disgrace to the family," said Parker.

"So the gas heater leak in the bathroom came at just the right time," said Turnbull.

"Mrs Stevens found her daughter's body and reported it to the police. They were suspicious, but there was no evidence," said Parker, reading off the computer.

"How convenient," said Turnbull.

Parker told Turnbull what he had found out about ghosts in computers.

"We know that ghosts appear in places where something terrible has happened," he said. "In the last five years there have been lots of reports of ghosts and frightening scenes appearing on computer screens."

"How could a computer do that?" asked Turnbull.

"Maybe the computer's electromagnetic waves pick up something in the room," he said. "Maybe Tracy's powerful brainwaves are sending her dreams to the computer screen."

"Do you think she's in danger?" Turnbull asked.

He nodded. "If Mrs Stevens has killed once, she could kill again."

"We must get Tracy out of this house as quickly as we can," Turnbull said.

Suddenly they heard footsteps in the corridor.
They rushed to their door but it had been locked.
When they tried to open the window they found
bars on the outside.

"We're trapped!" said Parker.

"We must get out!" shouted Turnbull.
"We must save Tracy!"

CHAPTER FIVE

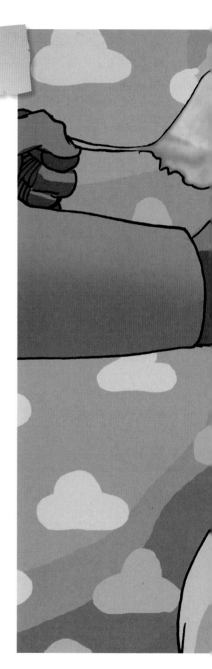

Meanwhile Tracy was in a deep sleep. She was dreaming about the long-haired girl who was screaming. Then she saw the door open and someone entered the locked room. She saw the face of the shadowy person — it was her grandmother!

Tracy woke up in a panic. She went to the computer and it came on. It showed the pictures in her mind. Then a shadow fell over the screen. A hand came down on her shoulder and a bag went over her head.

The agents banged and kicked at their door.

"Kick harder, Parker," shouted Turnbull.

"You're the martial arts expert, Turnbull," he snapped back.

They both sat down, exhausted.

"Give me your make-up bag," he said.

He looked through it until he found what he wanted.

"You want my nail scissors?" she asked.

He put them into the door lock.

"This is what they do in The X Files," he said.

"The trouble with you, Parker, is that you watch too much TV!" she said.

Suddenly the lock clicked and they fell through the door.

"The trouble with you, Turnbull, is that you don't trust your partner!" he replied.

They ran up the stairs.
Tracy's room was empty.

"We're too late!"
groaned Turnbull.

Parker went to the
computer. "Maybe Tracy
has used her special
powers to leave us
a clue," he said.

He was right.
The computer screen
showed a picture of a
young girl with a bag
over her head.

As they watched, the pictures changed to show
the bathroom.

They ran out of the room.

"She's going to carry out the same crime twice!"
Parker shouted.

When they got to the bathroom, the door was locked.

This time, Turnbull kicked it down. They found Tracy
in the bath. She seemed to be in a deep sleep.
They pulled her out and she was still breathing.
Parker found a suicide note in her pocket.

"Dear Grandma, I did not want to go on living.
The dreams are too much for me. Nobody can help
me," he read aloud.

Turnbull hugged Tracy. "What a terrible lie! We must
catch that wicked old woman," she said.

"You won't have to catch me, Agent Turnbull.
You're not going anywhere," a voice called out.
Mrs Stevens had come into the room, with a gun.

It all happened so quickly. Before Turnbull and Parker
could put their hands up, Tracy jumped up and rushed
at her grandmother.

One shot went off, hitting Tracy. Turnbull kicked the gun out of the old woman's hand while Parker grabbed the shower. He aimed the jet of water at Mrs Stevens's face, blinding her.

Parker handcuffed Mrs Stevens while Turnbull gave Tracy emergency first aid.

Parker used his mobile. "Get me an ambulance quickly. We have a gunshot wound," he commanded.

When they took Tracy away she was pale and grey. Turnbull was in tears.

"I don't know whether she'll live or die," she sobbed.

"We did the best we could," Parker said.

CHAPTER SIX

The two agents went back to the office. They had to write a long report for Commander Watson.

Parker sat down at the computer. Turnbull walked up and down the office.

"I can't write anything until I know if Tracy will pull through," she said.

"We must be careful what we say in this report," said Parker. "MI5 will never leave Tracy alone if they know about her special powers."

"That's the last thing she needs," Turnbull said. "She must be given the chance of a normal childhood."

The phone rang. It was the hospital. Parker took the call. He put the phone down.

"Laura, she's going to pull through," he said.

Turnbull jumped for joy. "Let's go and see her," she shouted.

Parker smiled at Turnbull. "Maybe you'd be a better mother than you think," he said.

"Maybe we should team up. We'd be the perfect parents," she joked.

Parker went very red.

At the hospital Tracy was sitting up in bed.

"I can't remember anything," she said.

"Do you remember your dream?" Turnbull asked.

Tracy shook her head.

"Do you remember the ghost in the computer?"
Parker asked.

"What ghost?" she said.

They looked at Tracy's medical notes and at the
machines showing her heart rate. All around Tracy the
computers were working. The world around Tracy was
normal again.

As they drove back to MI5, Turnbull scratched her
head. "Tracy seems to have lost her special powers,"
she said.

"So we don't have to write about them in the report,"
Parker said. "That means she'll be safe."

"It was incredible," Turnbull said, "seeing that ghost in
the machine. Seeing the story of Tracy's dead mum on
the computer."

Parker nodded his head. He didn't tell Turnbull that he hadn't seen the ghost in the computer. He didn't tell her that it wasn't just Tracy who had special powers. He kept secret what he had known for nearly a year about the strange object in Laura's skull. An object that had appeared after she had been in hospital for a foot operation.

Parker wondered who had put it there and why. He had a horrible feeling that one day he would find out. Until then, he was in no hurry to discover what was really going on.

GLOSSARY OF TERMS

broken the ice
to become friends

computer crashed
computer stops working

data information

disgrace to bring shame
on the family

electromagnetic waves
force which combines
both electricity and
magnetism

get on her nerves
to irritate her

leads clues

little madam nuisance

martial arts fighting skills

MI5 government
department responsible
for national security

nightmare a bad dream

out of order behaving
badly

Secret Service
Government Intelligence
Department

sick to death of me
fed up with me

sidekick close friend
or colleague

suicide note a note from
a person which says
that they intend to kill
themselves

QUIZ

1 What is the name of the girl who has nightmares?

2 Why does she live with her grandmother?

3 Why could she be a threat to national security?

4 What are the names of the Secret Service agents?

5 How did Tracy's mum die?

6 Who do the police think killed Tracy's mum and why?

7 What did Parker use to open the door from the agents' bedroom?

8 How did Tracy get wounded?

9 What did the agents have to write for Commander Watson?

10 How did the agents know that Tracy had lost her special powers?

ABOUT THE AUTHOR

Paul Blum has taught for over 20 years in London inner-city schools.

I wrote The Extraordinary Files for my pupils so they've been tested by some fierce critics (you!). That's why I know you'll enjoy reading them.

I've made the stories edgy in terms of character and content and I've written them using the kind of fast-paced dialogue you'll recognise from television soaps. I hope you'll find The Extraordinary Files an interesting and easy-to-read collection of stories.

ANSWERS TO QUIZ

1 Tracy Stevens

2 Because her mother is dead

3 Because computers crash when she is beside them

4 Agent Laura Turnbull and Agent Robert Parker

5 She drowned in the bath because the gas heater leaked

6 They think Mrs Stevens killed Tracy's mum because she brought disgrace on the family because she had a baby without being married

7 Turnbull's nail scissors

8 Mrs Stevens shot her

9 A report

10 The computers didn't crash around her